HoRRibLe HaiRCUT

Other titles in the bunch:

Big Dog and Little Dog Go Sailing
Big Dog and Little Dog Visit the Moon
Colin and the Curly Claw
Dexter's Journey
Follow the Swallow
"Here I Am!" said Smedley
Horrible Haircut
Magic Lemonade
The Magnificent Mummies
Midnight in Memphis
Peg
Shoot!

Crabtree Publishing Company
www.crabtreebooks.com

PMB 16A, 350 Fifth Avenue
Suite 3308
New York, NY 10118

616 Welland Avenue
St. Catharines, Ontario
Canada, L2M 5V6

Ritchie, Alison.
  Horrible Haircut / Alison Ritchie ; illustrated by Ian Newsham.
    p. cm. -- (Blue Bananas)
  Summary: When Mom decides to cut Lucy's long, tangly, messy
hair, the activity becomes quite an adventure.
  ISBN 0-7787-0844-6 -- ISBN 0-7787-0890-X (pbk.)
  [1. Hair--Fiction. 2. Haircutting--Fiction.] I. Newsham, Ian,
ill. II. Title. III. Series.
PZ7.R51155 Ho 2002
[E]--dc21

                2001032443
                LC

Published by Crabtree Publishing in 2002
First published in 2000 by Mammoth
Text copyright © Alison Ritchie 2000
Illustrations © Ian Newsham 2000
The Author and Illustrator have asserted their moral rights.
Paperback ISBN 0-7787-0890-X
Reinforced Hardcover Binding ISBN 0-7787-0844-6

3 4 5 6 7 8 9 0 Printed in Italy 0 9 8 7 6

HORRIBLE HAIRCUT

Alison Ritchie

Illustrated by Ian Newsham

BLue Bananas

To my hairdresser
A.R.

To Wendy and Mint
I.N.

Lucy had long hair. Lucy liked
her long hair.

She liked her hair

long and tangled and messy.

Her mother didn't.

And her father didn't.

"Lucy!" her mom said.

"You look like a hyena."

"Good!" said Lucy.

"Lucy!" her dad said. "You look like

a baboon!"

"Even better!" said Lucy.

"I think Lucy looks like Scruffy!" said

Lucy's brother Johnny.

"Perfect!" said Lucy.

"Time for a haircut!" said Mom

and Dad together.

"No! No! No!" said Lucy, running

out of the room and up the stairs.

"Yes! Yes! Yes!" said Lucy's mom,

grabbing the scissors.

"Come on, Lucy!" Mom shouted.

"Come downstairs."

"No! I don't want my hair cut!"

"Come down NOW!"

"Promise you won't cut off too much?"

said Lucy.

"I promise!" said Mom.

"Promise you'll stop when I say so?"

said Lucy.

"I promise!" said Mom.

"Promise you'll make it look nice?"

"Oh Lucy! Yes! Look, if you don't like it,

then you can cut mine, OK?"

"I can cut your hair if I don't like mine?"

asked Lucy. "Promise?"

"PROMISE!" said Mom.

"I'll only cut this much!

Just so it looks neat,"

said Mom.

"Mom," Lucy scowled. "I told you.

I don't want to look neat!"

Mom combed Lucy's hair. Then

she sprayed it with water, to

make it easier to cut.

"Now sit still, keep your head straight and don't make a fuss!"

Mom cut off a little bit of hair.

Mom cut off a little bit more hair.

Mom cut off even more hair.

Johnny tried to
trim Scruffy's fur.

He trimmed his ear instead.

Scruffy howled very loudly . . .

and very suddenly.

Mom jumped in surprise.

Mom's hand slipped. She cut off a very
big chunk of Lucy's hair.

"Oh, Scruffy! You made me jump. NOW
look what I've done."

"What? What have you done, Mom?"

said Lucy.

"Um, nothing, everything's just fine.

Johnny, leave the dog alone!"

"Now, let's see. Um . . . I just need to . . . er . . . sort of even it all up."

Lucy looked at the big pile of hair on the floor.

"STOP!" Lucy jumped up. She ran upstairs to look in the bathroom mirror.

Lucy ran into her bedroom and threw herself on the bed.

"Mom! It's horrible! It's awful!

I hate it! What am I going to DO?

I'm not going to school tomorrow.

I'm not going to school ever again.

Everyone will laugh at me."

"Of course they won't! Don't be silly!"

"Mom! You don't understand!"

"Look, your real friends won't laugh, and if anyone else does, just say your silly mother cut your hair too short! Anyway, a lot of your friends have short hair."

"But they've always had short hair,"
said Lucy. "This is new!"
"Well, it's not that bad!
Come on, let's see
what we can do."

"Now! We could curl it all up.

Or tie it up

Or mess it up

or even . . . wear a bow!"

"That's it! Now I'm cutting your hair,"

Lucy said, dragging Mom downstairs.

"OK, Mom. Ready?"

"Well . . . now, Lucy, you see,

the thing is . . ."

"You said!"

"Well, yes, sort of, but . . ."

"You promised!"

"OK! Sit still!" Lucy said. "Okay, here I go."

A promise is a promise...

There was a loud

SNIP!

Mom jumped up. She raced upstairs.

She screamed.

Dad came running up the stairs.

He looked at Lucy.

"Oh Lucy! Your hair looks

very er . . . um . . . interesting."

Then he saw Mom. He didn't

know quite what to say.

"How can I go to work tomorrow?" Mom wailed. "Everyone will laugh at me! What am I going to do?!"

"Don't worry, Mom," said Lucy. "It's fine. Just like mine!"

Lucy was beginning to feel a bit better.

"Oh dear," said Dad. "I suppose you could wear a hat?"

"That's not funny!" shouted Mom.

"Come on, Mom. It's not that bad. Maybe hats *are* a good idea!"

"I know!" said Lucy. "I've got a better idea!"

"Well, what do you think, Lucy?" said Mom, who was getting used to her new hair.

Lucy grinned, "You look like a hyena," she said.

"That's funny," said Mom, "So do you."

"Hurray!" said Lucy.

"Well, honestly! I live in a house full of
Scruffys!" Dad laughed.

"Speaking of Scruffy, where is that silly
dog?" said Mom.

"And where's Johnny?" said Dad.

"There they are!" said Dad.

"I'm sure they're up to no good!"

said Mom. "Come out, you two."